GW01071939

In the year 2065, se......................un-
teed for everyone o.........................ut
Security Patrol. Led by the resourceful Commander
Shore, W.A.S.P. exists to combat threats to world
peace.

Threats such as that posed by Titan, tyrant of the
ocean bed, overlord of the inhuman Aquaphibians. He
has sworn to destroy W.A.S.P.'s base at Marineville,
leaving himself undisputed master of the seas.

Pride of W.A.S.P.'s futuristic fleet is Stingray, the
state-of-the-art submarine. Stingray is captained by
Troy Tempest who, along with his loyal first officer,
Phones, is always on the alert to foil evil under the
sea. And they are aided in this mission by Marina,
maiden of a strange undersea race, who was Titan's
slave before rescue by Troy and Phones.

Back at base, they can always count on support
from Atlanta, the commander's strong-willed
daughter, and other stalwarts such as Lieutenant
Fischer, who mans Marineville's control tower.

Together, they form W.A.S.P.

Also available in
the STINGRAY series,
and published by Young Corgi Books:

TRAPPED IN THE DEPTHS
MARINEVILLE TRAITOR
THE DISAPPEARING SHIPS

STINGRAY: THE LIGHTHOUSE DWELLERS
A YOUNG CORGI BOOK 0 552 52781 5

First publication in Great Britain

PRINTING HISTORY
Young Corgi edition published 1992

STINGRAY © 1992 ITC ENTERTAINMENT
GROUP LTD. LICENSED BY COPYRIGHT
PROMOTIONS LTD.

Text copyright © 1992 by Transworld Publishers Ltd.
Cover and inside artwork by Arkadia.

Conditions of Sale
1. This book is sold subject to the condition that
it shall not, by way of trade *or otherwise*, be lent,
re-sold, hired out or otherwise *circulated* without the
publisher's prior consent in any form of binding or
cover other than that in which it is published *and
without a similar condition including this condition
being imposed on the subsequent purchaser*.
2. This book is sold subject to the Standard
Conditions of Sale of Net Books and may not be
re-sold in the UK below the net price fixed by the
publishers for the book.

Set in 14/18pt Linotype New Century Schoolbook by
Phoenix Typesetting, Burley-in-Wharfedale, West
Yorkshire.

Young Corgi Books are published by Transworld
Publishers Ltd, 61-63 Uxbridge Road, Ealing,
London W5 5SA, in Australia by Transworld
Publishers (Australia) Pty. Ltd, 15-23 Helles
Avenue, Moorebank, NSW 2170, and in New
Zealand by Transworld Publishers (N.Z.) Ltd,
3 William Pickering Drive, Albany, Auckland.

Made and printed in Great Britain by
Cox & Wyman Ltd, Reading, Berks.

STINGRAY

THE LIGHTHOUSE DWELLERS

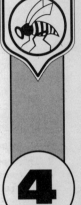

WASP

Dave Morris

4

YOUNG CORGI

THE LIGHTHOUSE DWELLERS

W.A.S.P PATROL

WASP

Crew : 2 , Captain and Hydrophone Operator
Power : Atomic Drumman WASP Hydrojet
Armament : Sting Missiles, Twin launchers

Ancillary craft:

TWO
Aquasprite, underwater 'jeeps'. On both port and starboard sides

ONE
Monocopter, stored in the aft upper cabin

page

A

1

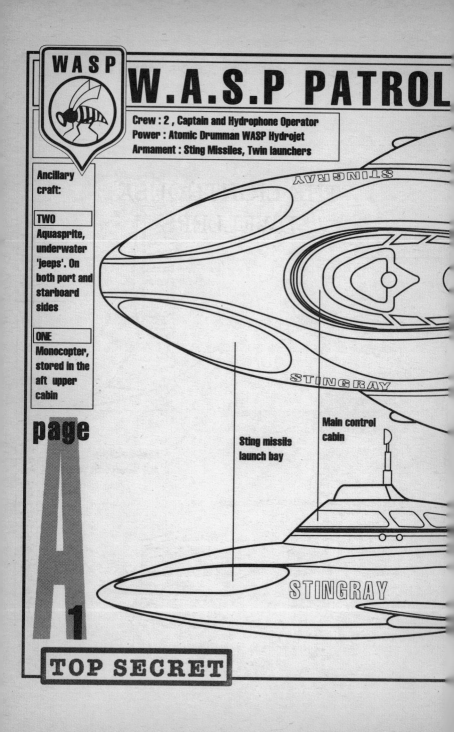

STINGRAY

STINGRAY

Sting missile launch bay

Main control cabin

STINGRAY

TOP SECRET

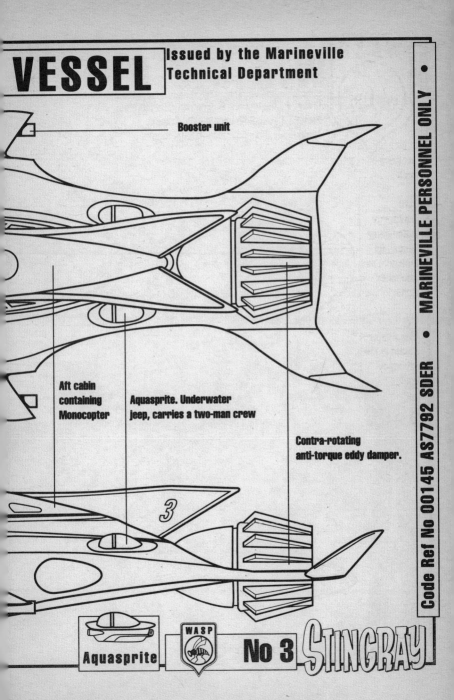

VESSEL

Issued by the Marineville Technical Department

Booster unit

Aft cabin containing Monocopter

Aquasprite. Underwater jeep, carries a two-man crew

Contra-rotating anti-torque eddy damper.

Aquasprite

WASP

No 3 STINGRAY

MARINEVILLE PERSONNEL ONLY • Code Ref No 00145 AS7792 SDER •

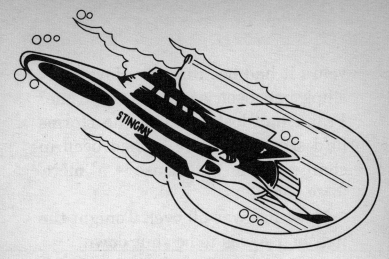

Chapter One
STORM BREWING

Thunder rumbled across the sky behind clouds the colour of charcoal. Frank Lincoln gazed out as the first droplets of rain spattered against the lighthouse windows.

'It's going to be a mighty big storm,' Frank muttered to himself.

He wondered how many storms the lighthouse had shone its beacon out into, during the hundred and seventy years it had been in use. How many ships had been saved in that time? Frank had lost count of the storms he'd seen just while he had been in charge of the lighthouse – a 'mere' forty years.

Now that was all over. Tonight the lighthouse was to be shut down.

A bleep came from the radio. Frank sighed. He had been expecting the call. Slowly he lifted the mike and flicked the radio switch.

'This is Marineville calling Arago Rock Lighthouse.' It was Commander Shore's voice.

'Hello, Commander,' replied Frank. 'Guess it's time, huh?'

''Fraid so, Frank,' said Shore over the radio. 'Are you ready?'

'As ready as I'll ever be,' said Frank.

There was a pause. Commander Shore knew how sad Frank was at having to close the lighthouse down. 'Thanks, Frank,' he said at last. 'Once it's done, I guess you can go home.'

'Home?' Frank chuckled bitterly. 'That's a laugh. My real home is here. Oh well, no sense in brooding about it. I'm going to shut down the power now. Arago Rock out.'

Frank snapped off the radio and wearily rose from his chair. He knew Commander Shore had been trying to cheer him up, but it was no good. How could he ever get used to the idea of leaving the lighthouse where he'd lived for the past forty years? He enjoyed the solitude, the sharp salty breeze and the rhythm of the sea.

If most people thought being a lighthouse keeper was boring – well, they were just wrong. There was plenty of excitement. The light had to be kept operating, flashing its warning message out to sea every seven seconds. Countless lives had been at stake over the years. Sailors who had never met Frank had seen his light, telling them to steer clear of the rocks. They owed their lives to his unflagging service.

Frank reached for the main power lever, hesitated a moment, then pulled it. The powerful beam of the main light faded. Only the soft red glimmer of the emergency lights remained on for Frank to find his way to the lift and descend.

At the door, he took a last look up the tower. Frank understood the need to shut down the light. A new airbase had been opened at Arago Point, nearby on the mainland. The lighthouse would have confused planes coming in to land. As for shipping – radar navigation was good enough these days that ships didn't need lighthouses to steer by anymore. Old-style lighthouses were out of date. Frank felt as if he was out of date, too.

Rain lanced down on Frank as he took his dinghy back to the mainland. Lightning crackled across the blackened sky. The storm was getting worse.

'Good job I didn't leave it another hour,' Frank said to himself; 'the outboard motor's barely coping with these high waves as it is.'

He took a last glance back towards the lighthouse. It stood dark and deserted against the storm clouds. Then, flying in out of the storm, he glimpsed a plane. The first to land at Arago Point. The herald of a new era.

In the cockpit of Sky Eagle 127, the pilot stared out through darkness and heavy rain. He could hardly see a thing. Strong winds buffeted his plane, and he was keen to get set down at Arago Point as quickly as possible.

He radioed the control tower: 'Arago Point, this is One-Two-Seven. Am I clear for landing?'

'Roger, One-Two-Seven. Runway approach lights now on.'

The pilot peered out into the night. He thought he could just make out the twin lines of lights marking the sides of the runway.

'Line up with the beacon for final approach, One-Two-Seven,' radioed the control tower.

A gust of wind brought a sheet of raindrops washing across the cockpit windshield. The pilot squinted and tried to catch sight of the runway again. But the downpour was too heavy; he could barely see anything at all.

Then a bright flashing light stabbed up out of the murk.

The light looked as though it was in the middle of the sea, but that must be an optical illusion, thought the pilot. It *had* to be the marker beacon. What else could it be? The pilot brought his plane in over the light, descending towards where he supposed the runway to be.

Down in his small dinghy, Frank Lincoln was horrified to see the lighthouse beacon suddenly come on! Even worse, the pilot of the incoming plane had obviously mistaken it for part of the runway circuit.

Frank jumped up in his boat and started waving his arms frantically. 'Pull up! Pull up!' he screamed over the shriek of the wind. 'You're going to hit the rocks!'

Of course, there was no way that the pilot could have heard him. The plane dropped down, streaking past the lighthouse tower at an altitude of no more than ten metres, and clipped its wing on a jutting spur of rock. The wing sheared off instantly, cartwheeling the plane over. It skimmed wildly across the waves, spouting flames, before sinking into the ocean about half a mile away.

Frank gasped. He thought he had seen the pilot eject at the last minute. He prayed he had.

He looked again at the lighthouse. The powerful beacon once more shone out from the top of the tower, just as it

had for the last hundred and seventy years.

Frank turned his dinghy around. He had to find out what had made the light come back on. Even more important, he had to make sure it was properly turned off before the next plane was due. And then he would look for the pilot of the plane who, if he had ejected in time, would need help in the raging sea.

He reached for the dock and tethered his dinghy. Inside, as he opened the door, he could hear the insistent bleep of the radio. No doubt Marineville had heard of the crash and wanted an explanation. Frank wasn't sure he could give one. Would they think it was his fault?

Frank's first priority was to shut down the light. He took the lift up to the top of the tower. The main light switch was only a few paces away, but he never reached it. A gun was suddenly pressed into his back and Frank heard an eerie non-human voice in his ear:

'Touch that light, and you die!'

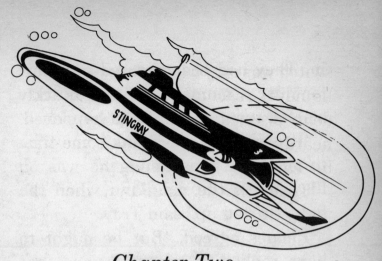

Chapter Two
DARK DOINGS

Back at Marineville, Commander Shore was keen to get to the bottom of things. The news about the plane crash had come in over the radio, but no-one had any explanation for why the lighthouse beacon had started up again.

'There's still no reply from the lighthouse radio,' said Atlanta.

Just then, Troy and Phones came

in. They had been ordered to report for duty. Commander Shore quickly briefed them on what had happened.

'It probably took Frank some time to get back – assuming he was on his way to the mainland when the light started up,' said Troy.

Phones agreed. 'But he ought to have replied to our radio messages by now,' he added.

'There's something strange going on out there,' said Commander Shore. 'As long as that light remains on, it's a danger to air traffic. Prepare to launch Stingray: I want that lighthouse investigated.'

In a very short time Stingray reached Arago Point. As they broke the surface, Troy and Phones saw high waves surging against the rocks ahead of them. Rain swept down out of the

24

night sky, rattling against the glass of the viewports.

While Troy put on a waterproof coat, Phones steered Stingray carefully towards the lighthouse. He had to be careful: just one mistake, and the heavy swell could send them dashing against the rocks.

Through the wash of water across the viewport, Phones spotted something brightly coloured. It was tethered outside the lighthouse, bobbing up and down with the waves. He peered. 'It's Frank's dinghy!' he suddenly realized.

Troy came over for a look. 'You're right. That means he's inside the lighthouse.'

'But in that case,' said Phones, 'why hasn't he turned the light off?'

'That's what I'm going to find out,' said Troy.

He took a torch that Marina handed
to him, then climbed up to the
main hatch. As he emerged on to
the conning tower, the storm winds
sent wave after wave of icy water
crashing into him. Troy held on to
the periscope shaft for support.

'This is as close as I can get, skipper,' said Phones over Troy's wrist-
radio.

Troy made his way out along Stingray's prow. Phones had done a fine
job, manoeuvering Stingray in between the high jagged rocks. Troy
easily leapt ashore.

He raised his wrist-radio to his
lips, having to shout over the growl
of thunder and the shrieking of the
wind. 'Moor Stingray right there,
Phones. I'm going inside.'

As Troy went up to the lighthouse door, he took a last look

back. He could see Marina standing beside Phones. Both were looking out at him through the darkness and rain, worried frowns on their faces. They seemed to sense the same thing he did: a feeling of something weird. Almost supernatural.

Troy chuckled to himself. He wasn't usually given to silly superstition – the storm must have spooked him, he decided. He touched the door. It swung open with a creak. A dull red light shone from inside the tower.

'Frank! Are you there? It's Troy Tempest!'

Troy's shouts echoed hollowly up the stairwell. He looked around. Assorted junk filled the bottom of the tower – barrels, packing crates, coils of rope, and spares for the lighthouse machinery. As Troy picked his way between all this, he noticed something else. There were some puddles of water across the stone floor.

So Frank certainly came back after the storm began, thought Troy. *Or* someone *did, at any rate.*

Troy spoke into his wrist-radio: 'Phones, Frank doesn't answer. I'm about to go up.'

'OK, Skipper,' replied Phones. 'Stay in touch.'

Troy opened the gate of the lift. Suddenly a loud bang rang out behind him. Troy whirled, instinctively dropping to one side in case of a surprise attack. But when he saw what had caused the noise, he felt very foolish. It was just the door blowing shut in the wind.

I'm even more spooked than I

thought, Troy decided. *Wonder how Frank stood it, living out here alone for years . . .?*

As the lift took him up to the beacon, Troy had another thought. What if Frank himself had come back to switch the light on? Everyone knew how bitter Frank had been when he was told about the lighthouse closing. And couldn't a person go a bit mad, spending years on their own in a creepy old tower like this, barely seeing another living soul from one month to the next?

Troy didn't like the idea. From the few times they had met, he'd always liked Frank Lincoln. He would hate to have to bring him in now. But as a wise precaution, Troy's hand dropped to the gun at his belt and he unclipped the holster flap.

The lift halted. Troy got out and

made his way around the curve of the wall towards the main power switch. Above him, the powerful beacon continued to sweep its dazzling beam out into the night.

Troy thought he heard something. 'Frank?' he said. 'Is that you? It's Troy Tempest.'

There was a movement just ahead as the beam swept by above. It looked like someone dodging back hastily out of sight. Troy barely glimpsed it against the glare. But by the time he stepped forward, the beam had moved on and his eyes could not adjust quickly enough to the gloom it left behind in its wake.

'Frank?' he called again. No reply.

As the beam swept round again, dazzling him, Troy decided he had better shut off the main power before he went looking for Frank. Not only

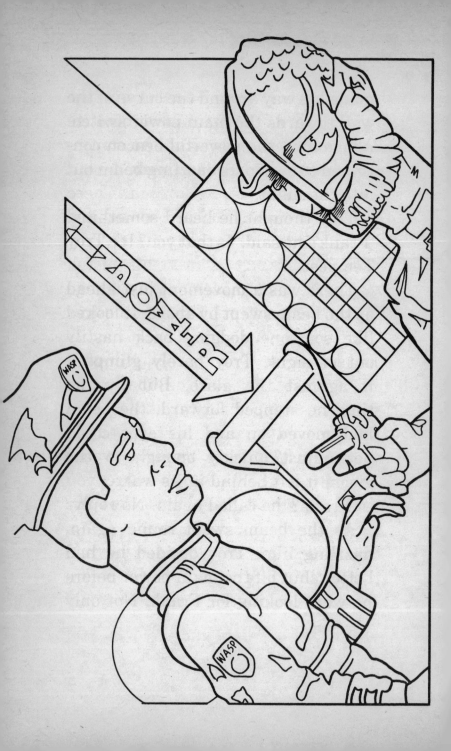

because the airfield couldn't operate until the light was off, but because Troy couldn't get used to the continual flashing of light and dark.

He reached for the switch. There was a rustle of damp clothing and a seaweedy smell in the air. Troy turned, making to draw his pistol, but he was confronted by a strange being with oily green skin and silver fronds instead of hair.

The creature held a raised gun. 'Give me your gun and that radio you wear on your wrist,' it said in a halting, chilly voice. 'And do not make any false moves. I would not hesitate to kill you, since you tried to turn off the light that my people need in order to live!'

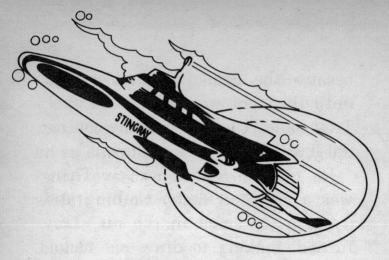

Chapter Three
LIGHT FANTASTIC

Phones wasted no time when he lost contact with Troy. He immediately called Commander Shore at Marineville for emergency instructions.

'Is the light still on, Phones?' came back Commander Shore's voice over the radio.

'Yes, sir,' replied Phones.

'Then get in there and switch it off,'

said the commander tersely. 'Troy must be in trouble.'

Phones pulled on a waterproof coat. 'You stay here,' he told Marina as he opened the hatch. 'Don't leave Stingray – and don't let anyone in unless Troy or I are with them.'

The hatch closed and locked. Phones hurried out along the prow and jumped over to the jetty. A gust of wind blew icy rain into his face, making him gasp for breath. He wrenched the lighthouse door open and darted inside.

Phones did not get as far as the lift. A strange figure stepped from the shadows behind a stack of crates. He had a gun, and he was pointing it directly at Phones's chest.

'Stop where you are, terranean,' hissed the stranger.

The dull red lighting gave Phones a good look at his captor. The creature was very much like a human, but thinner and perhaps a little shorter than an average man. The biggest difference was his skin – instead of normal flesh, his was gold-green in colour, and it glistened wetly in the light. And where a man might have had hair and a beard, it had straggly fern-like silver strands.

'You're a really ugly underwater alien, aren't you?' said Phones.

'Quiet,' ordered the creature. He waved his gun. 'Move over to the centre of the floor.'

Phones glanced across the stair-well. A space in the middle of the floor had been cleared of any junk. Did the creature mean to shoot him? No, he decided – he'd be dead already if so. He judged the distance between the two of them. He could never hope to leap and wrest the gun away before the creature fired. And others of the creature's race must already be holding Troy captive . . .

Reluctantly, Phones raised his arms over his head and walked to the middle of the floor. The strange creature followed him, keeping the muzzle of the gun trained on his back.

They stood in the centre of the room. 'Well?' said Phones.

'Wait,' said the creature.

A moment later, there was the faintest of clicks and then a circular section of the floor began to lower, carrying them with it. Phones had not even spotted the crack that marked the position of this concealed lift platform.

The lift descended down a circular shaft, burrowed deep into the rock on which the lighthouse stood. 'We are now below the level of the sea,' said the creature, confirming what Phones had already suspected. 'But there is air, so you need not fear for your life. Not yet.'

The shaft opened out into a large hall lit by regular pulses of green-tinted light. Pillars of polished coral supported a roof decorated with mother-of-pearl. As the lift continued down to the floor of this room, Phones was pleased to catch sight of Troy and Frank Lincoln. They were in chains, but looked unhurt.

'Phones!' said Troy. 'They got you, too.'

'Yeah, Troy,' said Phones, stepping off the platform. Immediately a couple of guards rushed forward and clamped chains on to his wrists. 'Who are these people?' Phones asked

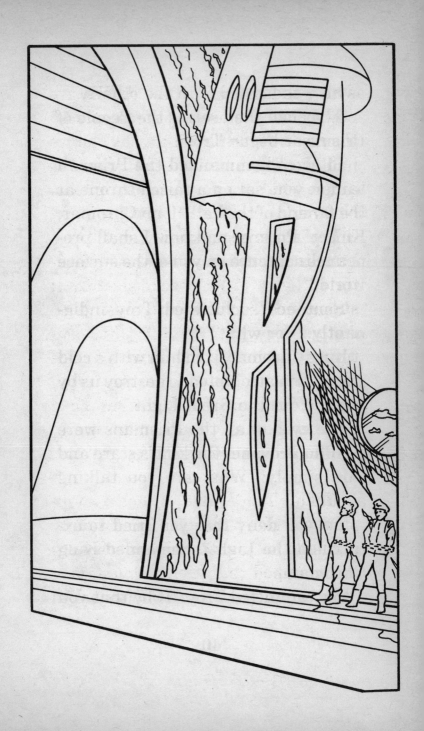

as he was herded with the others.

'They call themselves the People of Prisma—' began Troy.

'Silence!' commanded the Prisman leader, who sat on a raised throne at the far end of the hall. 'I am Chromar, King of Prisma, and now I shall pronounce sentence on you of the surface world.'

'Sentence!' spluttered Troy indignantly. 'For what?'

King Chromar fixed him with a cold glare. 'You attempted to destroy us by putting out the Great Light.'

The eyes of all the Prismans were on him. Troy met the king's stare and said simply: 'What are you talking about?'

'Do you deny that you tried to extinguish the Light?' demanded King Chromar.

'No,' admitted Troy. 'If by that you

mean the lighthouse beacon. But what has that to do with you?'

One of the Prisman guards – the one who had brought Phones down – pointed an accusing finger. 'Without the Light we would all perish!' he snarled. 'All our people would have been dead within a week, thanks to you terraneans!'

'I just don't understand,' muttered Phones. 'How can one lighthouse be so vital to you?'

King Chromar stroked the silver fronds of his beard. A new look had crept into his gaze: one of doubt. Perhaps he realized they genuinely knew nothing about the importance of the lighthouse to the Prismans. 'I will show you,' he said.

Touching one of a row of crystal buttons on the arm of his throne, the Prisman king caused a long

ornamental panel to slide open in the wall behind his throne. They could now see a huge glass window, beyond which the sea bed was murkily visible. Every seven seconds, a bright light shone down through the water – a dazzling white beam sweeping across the underwater sands.

'The lighthouse beam,' said Frank.

'Yes,' said King Chromar, rising from his throne and pointing through the window. 'And watch the anemones growing on the sea bed. See how they respond to the light.'

It was true. Each time the beam moved by, the sea anemones opened up to receive its light. As it moved on, leaving them in gloom, they closed again. An endless cycle of movement in the silent watery depths.

'The anemones depend on the Great Light,' explained Luxal, the guard who had spoken out before. 'And our people depend on the anemones for existence. Without their sustenance, we would sicken and die.'

'It's astounding,' said Frank. 'These people have been living under my lighthouse for years, and I never knew it.'

Troy nodded. 'And what it boils down to is, the lighthouse is as important to them as the sun is to us.'

King Chromar stood with his back to them for a few moments, head bowed and hands clasped behind his back. He seemed to be pondering the matter. Then he turned, and they saw that he had reached a decision.

'Now it is time to pass sentence,' he intoned.

Back aboard Stingray, Marina was getting more worried by the minute. With no message from either Troy or Phones, she had begun to suspect the worst. She would have swum over to the lighthouse to look for them, but she knew that whatever had befallen them might also happen to her. She could be more use to them by staying aboard as Phones had told her. That way she could at least radio Marineville for help.

Marina flicked on the radio, then

shook her head in frustration. How could she let Commander Shore know what was happening? She couldn't even speak.

The radio crackled. After a while, Atlanta's voice spoke: 'Marina, is that you? Is there anyone aboard Stingray?'

Marina did the only thing she could. She picked up the microphone and tapped it with her fingernails.

'I think it's Marina, father,' she heard Atlanta say.

Then Commander Shore took over. Marina found his gruff voice oddly reassuring. 'Listen, Marina,' he said, 'I want you to give one tap for "yes" and two taps for "no". Have you heard from Troy and Phones?'

Marina tapped twice.

'And is the light still on?'

She tapped once.

'Right,' said Commander Shore. 'We'll have to shut off the power from here. I'll have a rescue launch sent out at once. Don't worry, Marina, help is on its way. Marineville out.'

The radio crackled and went dead. Marina looked up at the flashing beacon. After a few seconds, it dimmed and went out. Commander Shore had done as he said – cut the main power supply. Marina allowed herself a faint smile. She somehow felt the light was the cause of all the trouble. Now that it was out, maybe Troy and Phones would be safe.

Under the ocean bed, Troy was just putting a proposal to the Prismans. 'We didn't know about your people,' he said. 'But now that we do, we'll do our best to help you. If you let us go, I guarantee that the light will stay on as long as it takes to arrange an alternative power source for you.'

The king considered this. 'Very well,' he said at last. 'We believe you, Tempest.' He gestured for the guards to step forward. 'Unchain the terraneans.'

At that precise moment, the light went out. Only a cold green glimmer remained in the long hall.

A shudder of dismay went through the Prismans.

King Chromar spun round and stared out through the window. He waited, but the light did not return. He turned back, and they saw that the harsh angry glare had returned to his eyes.

'Treachery!' he thundered. 'You tried to trick us, but now I see that you intended all along to deprive us of the Great Light! Now you will be destroyed!'

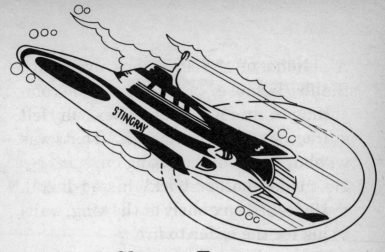

Chapter Four
SAVING BEACON

Even as the Prisman guards raised
their guns to shoot, Troy remained
calm. 'Now hold on,' he said loudly,
speaking to all the Prismans in the
hall. '*We* know why the light failed,
so we can repair it.'

'But, Troy,' Phones whispered,
'if the main power's been cut at
base, there's nothing we can do from
here . . .'

None of the Prismans overheard this because of the general commotion in the hall. They all felt they were doomed now. That was what Troy was counting on.

'It is another trick!' hissed Luxal. He looked anxiously at the king, waiting for the order to fire.

'You have to trust us,' insisted Troy. He turned to address the king directly: 'We're your only hope now. If you kill us, your people definitely will perish.'

The king nodded slowly. Troy could see his words were getting through. 'This man was the lighthouse keeper,' he went on, pointing at Frank. 'Let him go. You can keep us as hostages. He'll repair the light for you.'

'Very well,' Chromar decided. 'He will have two hundred and fifty Light flashes to do the work. If he does not succeed by then – or if he fails to return – you two will die.'

'Two hundred and fifty flashes . . .' murmured Phones. 'How long's that?'

'I reckon it's about thirty minutes, our time,' said Frank. But he knew if the main power had been cut at Marineville, he'd never be able to restore the light in time. He wasn't sure what Troy expected him to do. As the guards pushed him towards the lift, he turned to look back at Troy: 'Repair work like this won't, er, be easy, you know.'

'Yes, it will,' Troy called after him as the lift ascended. 'We do it *aboard Stingray* all the time.'

Frank was left alone in the lighthouse as the guards returned to Prisma on the lift platform. 'Remember what will happen to your friends if you fail,' grated one of the guards unpleasantly as he sank out of sight below the floor.

Frank wiped the sweat off his brow. Just what had Troy meant by that remark about 'aboard Stingray'? Obviously he'd said it that way because he knew the Prismans wouldn't pick up on what he had planned. But Frank wasn't sure that *he* understood either.

Then it came to him in a sudden flash. 'Of course!' he said aloud.

Instead of going up to the top of the lighthouse, he rushed to the door and wrenched it open. Gale-force winds whipped the waves up, smashing them against the rocks. Frank braced himself against the icy spray and peered out into the night. Stingray had broken her moorings and drifted off some distance. Cursing the extra delay, Frank jumped into the dinghy and started up the outboard motor.

The little boat started to push through the high waves, swaying this way and that. Frank aimed for where he could see Stingray bobbing up and down on the swell. There was somebody inside, looking out at him through the rain. At least that meant he wouldn't have any trouble getting inside, thought Frank.

He was wrong. When his dinghy arrived at Stingray, Marina refused to open the hatch for him. Frank clung to the outside and kept tapping on the thick glass of the viewport, but Marina just looked at him and shook her head obstinately.

'Come on, ma'am. Let me in – please!' yelled Frank. He wasn't even sure she could hear him over the constant growl of thunder. He glanced at his watch. More than fifteen minutes gone already! He had to get inside Stingray somehow.

He pulled a pad of paper from his pocket, and scrawled a note in pencil. The pad was utterly sodden in seconds, but Frank pressed it against the glass and prayed it would do the trick

Troy sent me. Needs help. Open hatch, read Marina from the pad. She looked out at the curious old fellow with the white beard, staring in at

her so urgently. Could he perhaps be the lighthouse keeper that Troy and Phones had spoken about? Marina was not sure, but she decided to risk trusting him. The rescue launch was still over an hour away, and she couldn't see any other hope of finding Troy. She unlocked the hatch.

Dripping water, Frank climbed down into Stingray. A look at his watch told him there was less than ten minutes left. He rushed over to the controls. Then he gave a gasp of dismay. There were more than a hundred different controls. How could he find the right one in time: the one that might save his friends' lives?

King Chromar's voice echoed stonily along the great undersea hall. 'Time is running out, terraneans. You have only fifteen Light flashes left.'

'Your friend failed you,' said Luxal, smiling as he checked his gun. 'Perhaps he fled, saving his own skin. But your lives will be forfeit.'

Phones leaned over to whisper to Troy: 'Frank might not be able to work out the controls, skipper. Maybe he didn't even understand what you wanted him to do.'

'Yeah,' Troy whispered. 'Either way, we'd better make a move soon or the Prismans will carry out their threat.' He strained at the chains holding his wrists. 'Uhh! – these chains are too strong. Can't break them . . .'

'Five Light flashes to go,' said Chromar, raising his hand imperiously. 'Guards – prepare to do your duty.'

The guards raised their weapons.

'Four . . .' the king counted, 'three . . .'

Troy stared around him, mind racing. There had to be *something* he could do. He couldn't just allow these underwater aliens to shoot them down in cold blood!

But time had run out. 'Carry out the sentence,' Chromar told the guards.

At that precise moment, a pulse of bright white light flashed through the hall. All the Prismans gasped,

turning to stare through the high glass window beside the throne. Outside, an intense beam of dazzling light was sweeping at regular intervals across the sea bed. The anemones gleamed with many colours as they opened to drink in the light.

'Then the old one succeeded,' said Luxal, lowering his gun. 'You are saved, terraneans.'

'We are all saved,' added the king, 'since, without the Great Light, we would have died, too.'

On the sea surface, aboard Stingray, Frank flicked a switch again. Stingray's main headlamps came on, casting bright beams down into the ocean depths. Frank counted seven seconds before flicking the switch off, counted another seven seconds and then flicked it on again.

'I hope Troy and Phones get here soon, ma'am,' he remarked to Marina with a grin. 'I can't keep this up all night!'

Sure enough, it was only a matter of minutes before Troy and Phones emerged from the lighthouse. Frank left Marina operating the headlamps while he took the dinghy across to pick them up.

'Whew!' said Frank when they were all aboard. 'I never thought I'd say it, but I'll be happy never to see this old lighthouse again.'

'But, skipper,' said Phones to Troy as they steered a course back to Marineville, 'what about the Prismans? Once we're out of the vicinity, they'll realize they've been tricked.'

'It's OK,' said Troy. 'I'll call Marineville and get them to prepare an *underwater* light beacon which we can place on the sea bed near Prisma. That will give the Prismans the illumination they need, but it'll be under the waves, so it won't be seen by aircraft.'

'So all's well that ends well,' said Frank. He ambled back to the standby lounge at the back of the cabin, sinking into the couch there with a sigh. 'Guess I'd better start getting used to my retirement. I don't really know what I'll do with myself, though . . .'

'Well, as to that,' said Troy, 'I'm not really supposed to say anything – it's Commander Shore's little surprise – but you might as well know now, Frank. They're giving you a job at the new airfield. You'll be in charge of the signal lights.'

'Really?' said Frank, a sudden broad smile creasing his weathered old face. 'That's great news, Troy! So it seems my new life won't be so bad, after all. And do you know – I think after all I won't miss that draughty old lighthouse one bit!'

THE END

STINGRAY TITLES AVAILABLE FROM YOUNG CORGI

THE PRICES SHOWN BELOW WERE CORRECT AT THE TIME OF GOING TO PRESS. HOWEVER TRANSWORLD PUBLISHERS RESERVE THE RIGHT TO SHOW NEW RETAIL PRICES ON COVERS WHICH MAY DIFFER FROM THOSE PREVIOUSLY ADVERTISED IN THE TEXT OR ELSEWHERE.

☐ 0 552 527785 **STINGRAY: TRAPPED IN THE DEPTHS**
Dave Morris £2.50
☐ 0 552 527793 **STINGRAY: MARINEVILLE TRAITOR**
Dave Morris £2.50
☐ 0 552 527807 **STINGRAY: THE DISAPPEARING SHIPS**
Dave Morris £2.50
☐ 0 552 527815 **STINGRAY: THE LIGHTHOUSE DWELLERS**
Dave Morris £2.50

All Young Corgi Books are available at your bookshop or newsagent, or can be ordered from the following address:

Transworld Publishers
Cash Sales Department
P.O. Box 11, Falmouth, Cornwall TR10 9EN

Please send a cheque or postal order (no currency) and allow £1.00 for postage and packing for one book, an additional 50p for a second book, and an additional 30p for each subsequent book ordered to a maximum charge of £3.00 if ordering seven or more books.

Overseas customers, including Eire, please allow £2.00 for postage and packing for the first book, an additional £1.00 for a second book, and an additional 50p for each subsequent title ordered.

NAME (Block letters) ....

ADDRESS..

....